The Kingdom
The Palace
Burth
Mermaid's Cove
Crestwood

of Wrenly
Flatfrost
Primlox
Bogburp
The Mainland
Hobsgrove

The Kingdom of Wrenly

11

The False Fairy

By Jordan Quinn
Illustrated by Robert McPhillips

LITTLE SIMON
New York London Toronto Sydney New Delhi

LITTLE SIMON
An imprint of Simon & Schuster Children's Publishing Division
1230 Avenue of the Americas, New York, New York 10020
First Little Simon paperback edition December 2016

Also available in a Little Simon hardcover edition.

For information about special discounts for bulk purchases, please contact Simon & Schuster Special Sales at 1-866-506-1949 or business@simonandschuster.com.
The Simon & Schuster Speakers Bureau can bring authors to your live event. For more information or to book an event contact the Simon & Schuster Speakers Bureau at 1-866-248-3049 or visit our website at www.simonspeakers.com.
Manufactured in the United States of America 1017 MTN
2 4 6 8 10 9 7 5 3
Library of Congress Cataloging-in-Publication Data
Names: Quinn, Jordan, author. | McPhillips, Robert, illustrator.
Title: The false fairy / by Jordan Quinn ; illustrated by Robert McPhillips.
Description: First Little Simon edition. | New York : Little Simon, 2016. |
Series: The Kingdom of Wrenly ; 11 | Summary: "A mysterious spell has hypnotized the fairies on the island of Primlox and it's up to Prince Lucas and Clara to save them"— Provided by publisher.
Identifiers: LCCN 2016021955 | ISBN 9781481485876 (hc) |
ISBN 9781481485869 (pbk) | ISBN 9781481485883 (eBook)
Subjects: | CYAC: Fairies—Fiction. | Magic—Fiction. | Princes—Fiction. |
BISAC: JUVENILE FICTION / Readers / Chapter Books. | JUVENILE FICTION / Fantasy & Magic. | JUVENILE FICTION / Action & Adventure / General.
Classification: LCC PZ7.Q31945 Fal 2016 | DDC [Fic]—dc23 LC record available at https://lccn.loc.gov/2016021955

CONTENTS

CHAPTER 1

Trick-and-Trip

"One orange honey blossom!

"Two orange honey blossoms!

"Three orange honey blossoms!"

Rainbow Frost and Amber Quill counted all the way to twenty-five orange honey blossoms—because that's how fairies count seconds on Primlox.

"Ready or not," cried the fairy sisters, "here we come!"

Then the two fairies darted through the island's forest. They peeked into squirrel holes and looked behind stumps and bushes. Amber Quill zipped across the forest path and bumped right into Falsk, a fairy who wasn't playing.

"Seen any fairies hiding?" asked Amber Quill hopefully.

Falsk had on a forest-green sepal petal skirt and wore a tiny hat of purple jasmine. She tapped the side of her head with one finger as if she were thinking. "Why, yes!" she whispered, pointing with her other finger. "I saw one right behind that tree."

Amber Quill tiptoed and jumped behind the trunk to surprise the fairy from her hiding place.

Ker-splat!

Amber Quill landed smack in the

middle of a mud puddle. *"Aaaah!"* she squealed. "I'm all splattered in icky muck!"

Falsk bent over, laughing. She watched Amber Quill stand back up. Her flower outfit was ruined.

"You tricked me!" Amber Quill said angrily.

Rainbow Frost landed beside Amber Quill. "That's because she's a *trickster* fairy," she said. "Never, *ever* trust Falsk. She wouldn't know the truth if it flew up and introduced itself to her!"

Amber Quill brushed the mud off her bluebell skirt. "I should've known better," she said with a whimper.

Falsk pulled out a handkerchief and waved it in front of Amber Quill. "Listen, I was only joking," she said. "No hard feelings, right?"

Rainbow Frost grabbed her sister's hand. "Come on!" she said hotly. "Let's keep playing with our *true* friends."

The fairy sisters flew far away from Falsk and went on with their game of hide-and-seek. They whizzed in and out of the branches, looking for their other friends.

Then Amber Quill spied something above the canopy of trees. "Look!" she cried, waving to her sister. "Some of our friends are up there. Let's get them!"

Amber Quill zoomed through the covering of leaves. Rainbow Frost followed close behind. Then the fairy sisters saw something strange. Their friends were flying in a flock, like birds. The two sisters called out, but none of the fairies answered.

"Something

is wrong," Amber Quill said. "They seem to be in a trance."

Rainbow Frost put her hand to her ear. "I hear music," she said.

Then Amber Quill stopped and listened. She heard the sound of a strangely bewitching flute. It played a song that the fairy instantly knew. She began to hum along with it. All at once, her eyes began to swirl and roll back in her head. Amber Quill fell into a deep trance as she floated skyward to chase the enchanted tune.

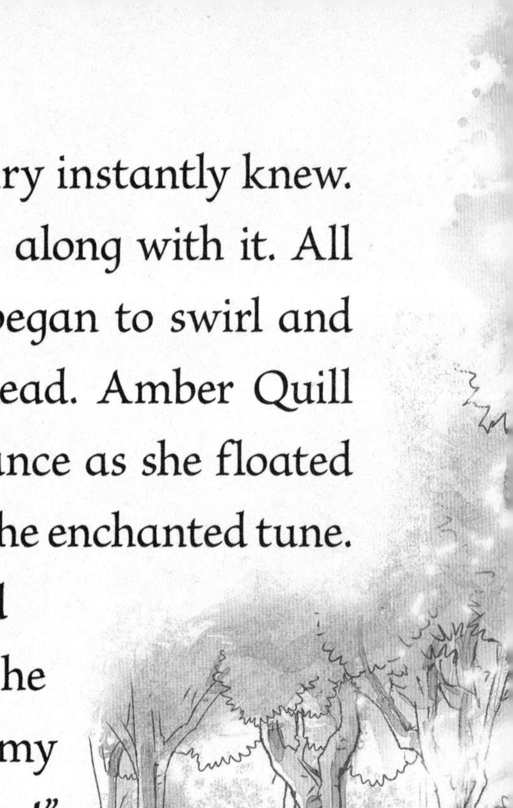

"Oh my!" cried Rainbow Frost. "The music has put my sister in a trance!" Rainbow Frost covered her ears with her hands. Then she flew toward the forest floor to escape the melody. All around her, one fairy after another fell under the musical spell and drifted up into the sky. Rainbow Frost touched down on the path and noticed Falsk stuffing milkweed fluff into her ears.

"Falsk!" Rainbow Frost cried. "The fairies are in troub . . . !"

Then a dreamy expression fell over Rainbow Frost's face. Her body began to float upward. Falsk

watched in horror as Rainbow Frost and the fairies of Primlox seemed to be pulled away by a dark, misty cloud moving across the sky.

"No!" cried Falsk. She searched the island for others, but no one was there. She was the last remaining fairy.

CHAPTER 2

Bull's-Eye!

Clara Gills pointed her bow toward the ground and prepared her arrow. Then she drew it, aimed, and released. *Thwack!* Her arrow stuck in the middle of the target.

"Bull's-eye!" she cried.

Prince Lucas smiled at his best friend. Then he grabbed an arrow from his quiver, took aim, and *twoof!* He hit the outer ring.

"My turn again!" Clara said gleefully.

She hit another bull's-eye. Ruskin, the prince's pet red dragon, squawked and flapped his wings.

"Whose side are you on, anyway?" Lucas complained.

Ruskin chirped happily. Lucas and Clara shot the rest of their arrows. Then they counted their points. Beyond the shooting area, there was a very long line of townspeople, trolls, and wizards outside the castle. Once

a month the palace was open to anyone who wanted to talk with the king face-to-face.

Lucas and Clara collected their arrows and slid them back inside their quivers.

"This time I'm going to beat you!" Lucas declared.

Clara laughed. "We'll see about that!"

The bushes beside the archery range rustled. Ruskin squawked sharply and began to sniff and paw at a hedge.

"Help!" cried a small voice from inside the bush. "Please, somebody, *help* me!"

"Stand down, Ruskin!" Lucas commanded. Ruskin backed away. "Good dragon."

Clara laid down her bow and crept over to the bushes. Gently, she pulled the branches apart where Ruskin had been pawing.

"Oh my!" Clara exclaimed. "It's a fairy!"

CHAPTER 3

The False Fairy

The fairy shielded her face with her arm. Her pearly wings flitted nervously.

Lucas knelt beside Clara and peered into the bushes. "Is everything all right?" he asked the fairy. Fairies didn't usually come to the mainland.

Falsk uncovered her eyes and shook her head. "My fairy friends are in trouble!" she cried.

Lucas tilted his head to one side. "What kind of trouble?" he asked.

Then Falsk explained how the sound of an enchanted flute had put the fairies into a trance. "They abandoned Primlox, following the music in a great swarm," she went on. "The strange song was coming from a dark, misty cloud moving across the sky."

Lucas and Clara looked at each other in surprise.

"You need to talk to the king," Lucas declared. "I can get you to the front of the line."

Falsk wrung her hands. "I can't. The king won't listen to me."

Lucas frowned. "What do you mean?" questioned the prince. "Come with me. I'll see to it he does!"

But Falsk couldn't look the prince in the eye. "I have a confession to make," she said sorrowfully. "I have a bad reputation in the Kingdom of Wrenly. I'm known as . . . the False Fairy."

Lucas and Clara both gasped.

"You're the legendary *False Fairy*?" Lucas exclaimed.

Clara shook her head in disbelief. "You made up the rumor about the Ghost of Wrenly!"

The children named rumor after rumor that Falsk had made up—stories of six-headed dogs, giant ice trolls, and bats in the schoolhouse.

"Okay, okay," said the mischievous fairy, squeezing her fists. "I *know*! I am a very *bad* fairy. The king and queen will never believe my story."

Clara wagged her finger at Falsk. "Why should anyone believe you?" she asked.

Lucas nodded. "Clara's right. For one thing, why are you the *only* fairy who hasn't been bewitched?"

Falsk held her hands over her ears. "Stop! Please!" she begged. "If you don't believe me, then come to Primlox and see for yourself."

And just like that Lucas and Clara had found their next adventure.

CHAPTER 4

Anybody Home?

The prince enlisted the crew of the *Royal Scepter,* one of the ships that took passengers from island to island in Wrenly, to help them on their mission.

Neither Lucas nor Clara believed there was any truth to Falsk's story. It sounded very far-fetched that all the fairies in Primlox were gone, but they set forth anyway.

Grom, one of the ruling wizards of Hobsgrove, also boarded the ship.

"What do you need in Primlox?" asked Clara.

Grom patted his leather satchel. "Potion ingredients," he said. "They are waiting for me at Queen Sophie's castle."

Lucas, who had been looking out on the water, became interested. "What kind of potions are you working on?" he asked.

Grom stroked his beard thoughtfully. "Let's see," he said. "Potions for bad-dragon-breath and stain removal, cough serums, and tracking spells."

"Let me know when you finish the bad-dragon-breath potion," Lucas said, pinching his nose and motioning a thumb at Ruskin.

Ruskin squawked.

"And what about you four?" Grom asked. "What brings *you* to the fairy island?"

Lucas and Clara explained what

Falsk had told them at the archery range. They also told him about her reputation.

Falsk hung her head. "But this time I'm *not* lying," she said.

Grom wrinkled his forehead. Even he didn't know what to believe. "Hmm. Perhaps, my prince, you would not mind if I joined you on this adventure?"

"The more the merrier," answered Lucas as the ship set sail.

After a short trip over calm

waters, they finally arrived. The ship docked, and the travelers headed for the fairy castle. Nobody greeted them in the great hall.

"Hmm . . . that's strange," Lucas commented.

Clara looked around. "Hello?" she called. "Queen Sophie? Anybody home?"

Nobody answered. The only sound in the castle was the lonely echo of Clara's voice.

They spread out and began to search for fairies. Clara checked

the bedrooms. Lucas looked in the library, the throne room, and the kitchen. Ruskin inspected the towers, while Grom investigated the cellars and storerooms where he also found some ingredients. They could not find a fairy in the whole castle.

“Hmm, come on. Let’s check the gardens,” Lucas suggested.

They ran over a stone bridge and through the evergreen archway. The flower gardens were empty. Not a single fairy was collecting nectar for honey. The orchards and hedge mazes were barren too.

Up and down the pebbled lanes the fairy cottages stood empty, and the front doors were wide open. Without the magical fairies, the island had begun to look dull and run-down.

"I told you!" said Falsk, hoping that now they would believe her story.

Lucas looked around the empty island. "Is this some kind of incredible joke?"

Falsk flittered around in dismay. “I’m telling the truth!” she wailed. “The fairies are under a musical spell and have been lured away by a dark, misty cloud. The only reason I didn’t fall into a trance was because I filled my ears with milkweed fluff when I saw what was happening.”

Clara looked at Lucas. “I’m beginning to believe her,” she said.

“Me too,” agreed Lucas.

CHAPTER 5

A Sign

Grom pulled his spell book from his satchel. "Maybe I can find an explanation for the musical trance in here."

Lucas nodded. "We must send for help from the king," he said.

They hurried back to the harbor, where another boat had docked.

An old fisherwoman walked toward them and shook her head. "I just saw the strangest sight," she said to the children, Falsk, and Grom, who still had his nose in his spell book.

"What did you see?" asked Clara.

"Hundreds of fairies flying after a strange dark, mystical cloud!" she exclaimed.

Lucas and Clara gasped.

"Which way were they headed?" asked Clara.

The fisherwoman pointed. "East," she said.

They thanked the fisherwoman and started down the dock toward their ship.

"Let's go!" Lucas shouted.

"Wait!" the fisherwoman called after them. "Before you set sail, I have something that may be of interest to you."

Lucas, Clara, Grom, and Falsk gave the fisherwoman their full attention.

The fisherwoman reached into her pocket and pulled out an object shaped like a teardrop. It was flat, and it shimmered in the sunlight. She handed it to Lucas.

"It looks like a dragon scale," he said, turning it over.

Ruskin sniffed the scale and

whined. Then Lucas showed it to Grom.

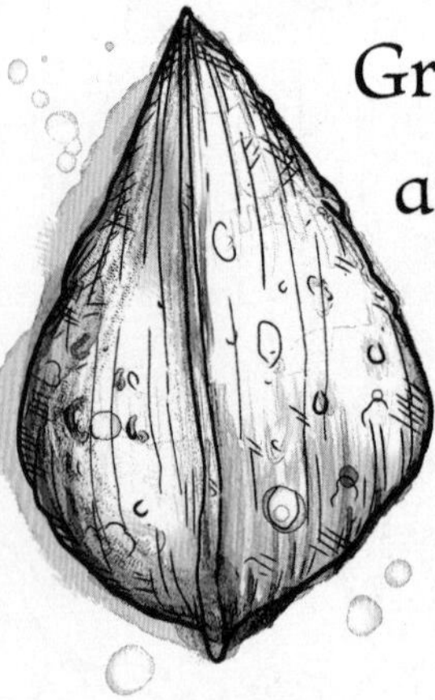

"I've never seen a scale this color," Grom said. It was silver, blue, and purple.

Clara inspected the scale too. "Is it a scale from a dragon or some *other* kind of creature?"

The fisherwoman looked up at the sky. "All I know is that the scale fell from the cloud the fairies were following."

Grom opened his leather satchel. "May I hold it for safekeeping?" he asked Lucas. "It may prove helpful in tracking the fairies."

"Of course," said the prince, handing over the scale. Then he thanked the fisher-woman and asked her to get word to the king that they were setting out on a mission to rescue the fairies.

Lucas turned to the others. "Well," he said, "it looks like we have ourselves a second adventure."

Clara smiled. "And I thought things were getting dull in Wrenly," she said, rubbing her hands together. "Let's go find those fairies."

Ruskin squawked his approval.

Grom frowned grimly. “Don’t kid yourselves, young ones,” he said. “This adventure could prove to be very dangerous. Very dangerous indeed.”

CHAPTER 6

Shapes in the Clouds

"We have no time to lose!" Lucas cried, running up the gangplank with the others close behind him.

They cast off and headed east in a blustery wind. The ship creaked and heeled to one side. Whitecaps foamed on the crests of the dark green waves. The sun poked out between clouds, and its rays shimmered like spotlights on the water.

Falsk stayed close to Clara, who leaned on the rail and studied the choppy water for clues.

"Do you think I'll ever see my fairy friends again?" Falsk asked sorrowfully. "What if the last thing they remember about me is how I tricked Amber Quill into jumping into a mud puddle?"

Clara looked the False Fairy in the eye. "You must think good thoughts and be strong for your fairy family," she said.

Falsk nodded as a tear rolled down her cheek. "If we do find the fairies, I promise I'll never play another prank for the rest of my life."

Then Clara held a finger to her lips. “Shh,” she said. “Do you hear something?”

Falsk listened. An eerie tune whistled in the wind.

Wooooooooooooooooooooooooooo . . .

Falsk knew instantly what this

bewitching sound meant. "That's the song that charmed the other fairies!" Swiftly she slipped her hand into her pocket and pulled out a tuft of milk-weed fluff to push into her ears.

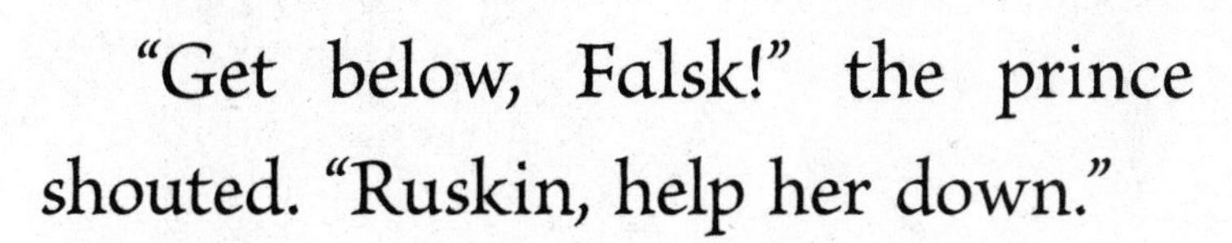

"Get below, Falsk!" the prince shouted. "Ruskin, help her down."

The red dragon led Falsk into the ship's cabin to get her farther away from the strange humming sound. Then he returned to deck.

Everyone else remained on alert. They studied the sea and sky for more clues. Soon their imaginations began to play tricks on them. Each wave seemed to swell with monster faces, and the clouds took on beastly shapes.

Lucas shinnied up the mast and climbed into the crow's nest attached to the masthead.

He put his hand to his brow, scanned the horizon, and spied a dark cloud. *There's something strange about that cloud,* Lucas thought. It was as if it had wings and a body.

The prince slid down the mast and reported his finding to Clara and Grom. They began to track the cloud too.

"I think that something is hiding in the cloud," said Lucas. "A creature, to be exact. And I'd bet anything that the scale we have belongs to it."

"It *is* moving faster than the other clouds," Clara noted.

Grom noticed it too. "And the whispering flute song is growing quieter as the cloud moves away."

Lucas gnawed on one of his knuckles as he watched the dark shape. "We'll never catch up to that cloud in this clunky old ship," he complained. "It's much too slow."

Clara sighed. "You're right," she agreed.

Grom opened his satchel and pulled out the scale the fisher-woman had given them.

"It's time we put a tracking spell on that creature in the cloud," he said.

Clara's face brightened. "That would be great, but it still doesn't solve the problem of our *slow* ship," she said.

Grom dropped the scale back into his satchel. "Our ship does need more power," he said. "Can you think of anyone right for the job?"

Lucas and Clara gave each other a puzzled look.

Then Lucas's eyes grew wide. "Do you mean Ruskin?"

CHAPTER 7

The Spell

"Is Ruskin strong enough to pull a ship?" asked Lucas.

"Probably not," Grom answered. "But he *could* pull a smaller boat."

Grom walked toward a large dory—a lifeboat—hanging from the side of the ship.

Lucas sized up the dory. "It's perfect!" he declared. Then he gave orders. "I'll lower the boat. You two get started on the tracking spell."

Grom and Clara hurried below and told Falsk and Ruskin the plan. Then Grom set a mortar and pestle on the galley counter. He opened his spell book and laid out the ingredients for a creature-tracking spell:

1 body part from creature to be tracked (hair, fingernail, scale, dander, or shell)
1 cup orange blossom honey
½ turnip
1 handful of gooseberries
1 swoosh of snail slime

Clara handed the ingredients to Grom one at a time.

"It's a good thing you had to pick up all these spell ingredients in Primlox today," Clara commented.

Grom cut the root from a turnip. "I'd say it was a good thing we *all* went to Primlox today."

The wizard ground and mixed the spell ingredients with the mortar and

pestle. Then he unclasped a silver medallion, which was also a locket, from around his neck and filled it with the potion. With all in place, Grom chanted the tracking spell.

Pursue-mora!

Pursue-a-meest!

Hot on the trail of an
unknown beast.

Track it down in a
high-speed chase.

Then make known its
hidden face.

POOF!

Sparkling light and glitter swirled from the locket. It rippled out of the cabin and up into the sea air.

Grom fastened the locket around Ruskin's neck.

"Follow me," Grom said to the dragon. "Falsk, stay below until I return."

Lucas, Clara, and Ruskin climbed into the dory. Grom handed them a

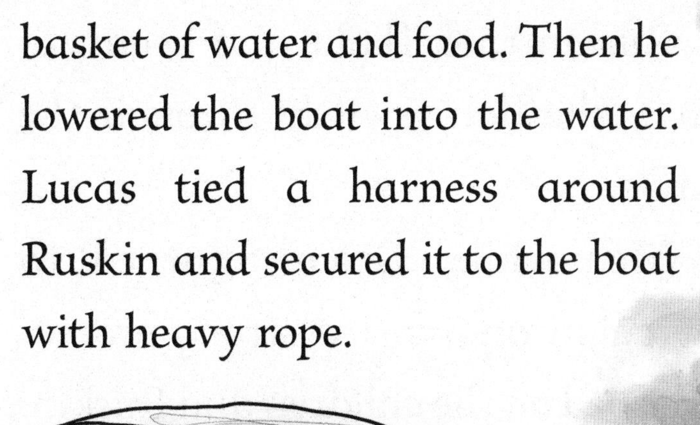

basket of water and food. Then he lowered the boat into the water. Lucas tied a harness around Ruskin and secured it to the boat with heavy rope.

Ruskin took flight and began to carry the dory swiftly through the waves.

Meanwhile, Grom returned to the cabin and cast a strong protection spell on the children and Ruskin. Then he told Falsk she could unstop her ears. "The humming is out of range for now," he said.

The frightened fairy pulled the fluff from her ears. "Is there a terrible monster out there?" she asked.

Grom heaved a great sigh. "The sound is coming from *some* kind of creature. But a terrible monster?" He paused. "Only time will tell."

CHAPTER 8

Rumblings

Stars dotted the sky like starry gems. The sea had calmed, and Ruskin pulled the dory quickly across the water. There had been no sight or sound of the creature since they had left the ship.

"We'll have to trust the tracking charm," Lucas said.

Clara nodded. "And our wits," she added.

Lucas and Clara took turns watching and sleeping. Ruskin took breaks for fish snacks and water every hour. Soon the sun began to rise.

Clara spied something in the distance. "An island!" she cried, pointing.

Lucas rubbed his eyes and sat up. Sure enough, there was a strip of land on the horizon.

"I never knew there was an island out here," said the prince. "It's definitely not on any map."

Ruskin flew faster, seeing land up ahead. Soon the boat scuffed along a sandbar. Lucas and Clara hopped into the shallow water and undid Ruskin's harness. Then they pulled the boat onto the beach. The morning sun felt warm on their backs. Ruskin squawked and ran toward the edge of a jungle.

"Come on!" Lucas said, following Ruskin toward the trees.

Ruskin sniffed out a path into the jungle. The path led them under a

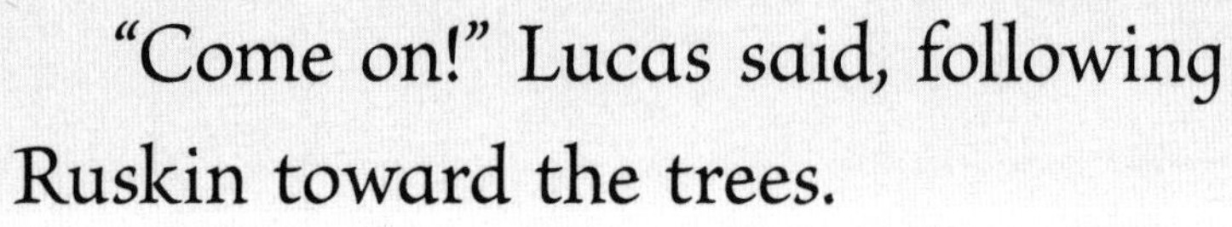

thick canopy of trees. Ruskin found a freshwater stream and splashed into it. He stood under a waterfall

and lapped the falling water. Lucas and Clara drank too.

Then they walked along the path lined with trees, vines, and flowering bushes. Insects clicked and buzzed in the branches.

"This island reminds me of Primlox," said Lucas. "It's so beautiful and lush."

Clara pushed a vine out of the way. "I wonder if it's fairy magic," she said.

Ruskin stopped and looked up into the umbrella of leaves. He barked loudly.

Lucas looked up and drew in a sharp breath. "There *is* fairy magic here!" he cried.

Clara leaned her head back. Several fairies flew overhead. The children spied Rainbow Frost, Amber Quill—even Queen Sophie.

"Hey! Down here!" Lucas called, beckoning with his hands.

Clara waved too. "Hello! Calling all fairies!" she cried.

The children shouted, whistled, and clapped their hands. But it was no use. The fairies didn't seem to hear a word they were saying.

"They must still be in a trance!" cried Lucas.

"Shh! Be quiet," Clara said. "I think I hear something."

Lucas stopped and listened. Something close by rumbled and rattled. It sounded like a wheeze . . . deep down inside the island's throat.

"It's coming from behind that

hanging moss," Clara whispered.

The thing rasped again, and Ruskin began to growl. Lucas put a hand on Ruskin's head to quiet him.

Then what sounded like claws scraped against rock, followed by a thunderous *Thwap! Thwap! Thwap!*

"That sounded like very large wings," whispered Lucas.

Clara looked at the prince. "What do you think it is?" she whispered.

Lucas shrugged. “Whatever it is, it’s *not* human,” he said quietly.

Then a twig snapped under Clara’s foot. The children froze. The creature grunted.

Lucas laid a hand on Clara’s shoulder. “Let’s find out what’s over there,” he whispered.

“Right behind you,” said his best friend.

CHAPTER 9

Trapped!

The children gently pulled back the curtain of moss and peeked between the branches. There stood a shimmering beast at the mouth of a dark cave. It had the body of an enormous dragon and the wings of a monstrous bat. Purple, blue, and silver scales neatly overlapped one another, like shingles, on the beast's body. The scales looked just like the one the fisherwoman had found. Two curved horns rose up from the crest of the beast's head, while thousands of hairy spikes ran down its back.

The tip of its tail curled like a snake.

Lucas blinked. "It's *huge,*" he whispered.

Clara swallowed hard. "Do you think it's friendly?" she asked uncertainly.

"I don't know about friendly, but it sure looks powerful," Lucas responded.

Ruskin barked.

"Shh!" Lucas shushed sharply, but it was too late.

The creature locked its glowing crystal eyes on all three of them.

Lucas dropped the curtain of moss to escape its stare.

"Bad boy, Ruskin!" he scolded. "We didn't even have a plan yet!"

Ruskin squawked and raised his wings. Then he flew through the drape of moss straight toward the creature.

"What's he *doing*?" cried Clara.

They peered through the moss. Ruskin landed in front of the creature and began to chirp and bark.

"He's trying to talk to the beast!" Clara said.

"We have to stop him!" cried Lucas.

Lucas and Clara flung back the moss and charged toward Ruskin. The beast fastened its gaze on the children and began to thunder toward them.

"Run!" Lucas yelled.

Lucas and Clara darted back into the jungle. The beast began to flap its heavy wings and took flight. Lucas and Clara kept going.

Then, from above the treetops,

they heard the eerie humming. It was the same sound they had heard from the ship, but it was much, much louder. Ruskin squawked overhead too. The children stumbled over plants and roots as they raced down the path. Then they burst out of the jungle onto the beach. They barreled toward the boat.

Then *whoosh!* All at once the enormous beast swooped down and landed on the beach in between the kids and the boat. The enchanted fairies of Wrenly swarmed around the great beast. The children froze.

"Oh no!" Lucas cried. "We're trapped!"

CHAPTER 10

Brave Little Wings

A fairy fluttered down from a palm tree above the children. She landed in the sand—directly in front of the creature.

Lucas and Clara looked at each other in alarm.

"It's Falsk!" Clara whispered.

The creature lowered its serpent face in front of the fairy. Falsk trembled wildly.

"I—I—I am Falsk," she began shakily, "the last fairy of Primlox, and this is Prince Lucas of Wrenly and his best friend, Clara."

The beast grunted and relaxed his wings.

"We mean you no harm," the brave little fairy went on. "We have come to gather my friends, these fairies who surround you, to bring them home."

Then, to everyone's surprise, the creature spoke.

"I know not of Wrenly," it said in a deep, gravelly voice. "The place where you stand is Siren's Island, and I am Siren. I sleep most of the time—sometimes for years. When I wake up, I go out in search of food. This time these tiny flying creatures followed me home. I know not why."

Grom, who had rowed in from the ship, stepped from his small boat and walked up the beach.

"I know why, great Siren of Siren's Island," said Grom. "The fairies of

Primlox have been bewitched by the hum of your spikes when you fly. The beautiful melody has put them into a trance."

Siren tipped his scaly chin toward Falsk. "How is it this one stays awake?" he asked.

Falsk knew the beast was talking about her, but she couldn't hear what he said. She looked to Grom.

"Her ears are filled with milkweed

fluff," he said. "It shields her from your bewitching song."

Siren nodded. "This tiny creature is brave to talk to a beast of my size. She had no way to know that I am friendly. I would like to call her Brave Little Wings."

Lucas, Clara, and Grom turned to Falsk and bowed their heads. The wee little fairy had risked her life to save them

all. Then Lucas stepped forward.

"She will be greatly honored," the prince said. "But tell us, how can we wake the fairies from their trance?"

Siren shook his head. "I know not

how to awaken them," he said.

"But I know," Grom said. "The fairies will wake up when they leave Siren's presence. Then there will be nothing to hypnotize them."

"I meant no harm," the ancient dragon apologized. "I cannot control my wing song. You must get the fairies back to their home."

Clara looked out to sea. "But we have no idea where we are."

Siren lifted his mighty head. "Then I shall lead you back," he said.

The travelers boarded the ship and sailed home. They followed

Siren's mystical cloud, which they had learned was his camouflage—a thick mist given off by his scales. The fairies trailed behind the dragon in a great swarm.

"Wait until our families hear

about this!" Lucas said as they sat in the cabin with Falsk, who had to stay away from the hum of Siren's spikes.

Clara cut a piece of oatmeal bread from a thick loaf. "More important, wait until the fairies hear that Falsk saved them all," she said.

Falsk fluttered close to Lucas and Clara. "Do you think the fairies will like me now?" she asked.

Lucas smiled. "That depends, Brave Little Wings," he said. "Have you become a trustworthy fairy?"

Falsk nodded firmly. "From now on, I will never play another trick," she said. "And I'll be truthful, honorable, and kind."

And this time everyone believed her.

Enter

For more books, excerpts, and activities, visit **KingdomofWrenly.com**!